Love
Truth
&
Travel

By
Marie Skilling

Love, Truth & Travel

Published by

Picouture Press

To Nanny Wales,

Thank you for everything.

```
                K
            N   I   D
        G   U   N   E   R
    I   R   R   D   S   E   E
    L   N   O   T   N   I   S   F   A
A   O   S   W   U   E   R   P   F   S   M
C   V   P       R   S   E   E   O   P   A
C   E   I       E   S       C   R   I   N
E       R                   T   T   R   I
P       E                       E   F
T                                   E
                                    S
                                    T
```

FOR THE LOVE & TRUTH OF IT!

YOU MATTER.

WE ALL MATTER.

Introduction

This book is a gift borne out of the life given to me.

I have been fortunate enough to experience amazing things, in incredible places, all over the world.

I have also known the not so nice side of life at times, as we all have. But in each of those experiences, I have been offered important lessons.

I am someone that processes my experiences through the written word, quicker than any other way I have tried.

However, the support of others has helped me to take huge leaps of faith, and shift the deeper stuff that sometimes gets in my way.

By sharing my poetic words with you, I hope to touch your heart and inspire you.

Life is out there for the taking, but it can sometimes feel like it's stringing us along.

It is during those times that it's important to take a moment to find kindness in our hearts and shine it inward.

Self-kindness is as important as being kind to one another.

I have been reminded of that many times.

And whether you're stepping into another culture, entering someone's life or sharing your opinion, do so with kindness.

Together we create community.

It is my hope that this book of poems creates a feeling of connection to remind you all that you are never alone.

Much Love,
Marie

LOVE

When you and I and the world are
young,
And all the sad songs are yet unsung,
The heart is filled with morning
laughter,
Without a care for what comes after.

Anon.

Ready to know you

I search for you within my dreams
Your face is only a shadow.

But I know it's you when you visit
me
By the way you make me feel.

Your hand on mine lets me know
you're alive
But where in this world, I don't
know.

So I sit with your presence to learn
who you are
To sense you when you arrive.

For the day will come when you step
into view
And when you do, I will welcome
you.

So make it known you're the one,
my dear
I'm ready to know you, let's make
that clear.

Setting me free

Your gentle deep affections
Stir me to my core
Unbinding all the mystery
You're dying to explore.

Delving into layers
Previously unknown
You're eager to discover
The who of whom I am.

Relaxed within your reach
I unravel in your arms
Feeling safe to share
As you listen with your heart.

Cherished little moments
Mean so much to me.

That you care to hear my story
Truly sets me free.

The Promise

My heart feels your beat
The rhythm of your soul
Your deeper reverie
And the things you see in me.

My gifts you do possess
But you are yet to see
The choice that they afford:
To close me or release.

Open up my being
With your strong but gentle touch
Melting all my armor
To set me fleeting free.

In return I'll meet you
Your mate in life's soiree
And gift you with my heart
Running deep for you always.

Walk with me in life
United and unique
Embracing all we are
And loving through our pain.

As passion fills the space
And laughter pokes the air
We'll love each other fairly
And bloom as we both care.

Lost in your love

My emotive heart runs wild
Racing through the minutes
Skipping beats upon paused breath
All sense vacates my mind.

Intellect abandons me
I lose my sense of self
Focused on your presence
My eyes see only you.

I hold you in my hands
And hope you know the words
That cannot leave my lips
For they have failed me.

My smile speaks the truth
For the love I have for you
In all the things you see
That seep from deep in me.

I wait for you to feel
The power you bestow
To open up my heart
Safely in your arms.

For you hold my soul
Loving all the way
As we drift along together
Bonding every day.

Palm of Truth

A letter of truth
Rests upon my open palm
Exposing my love for you.

Feel the message it shares
For my soul speaks louder through
the skin of my hand
Than any pen can say.

The meaning is true
That I share with you
From the depths of my loving heart.

Yours

Your touch possesses me
Your warmth embraces me
Your laughter draws me in.

Your eyes beckon me
Your lips devour me
Your scent makes me spin.

Your breath caresses me
Your body holds me
You can only win.

Home of hearts

There lives a spirit within these walls
Far greater than the air that breathes
It stirs foundation's frosty ghosts
From hiding shame beneath.

A writer's love from days gone by
Stirs amongst the breeze of time
Singing on the strings of love
Holding notes of hope.

A window of forgotten pasts
Reveals a fire that's now run cold
As emptiness surrounds the frame
Where golden gifts were once
behold.

Winter snows frost the glass
As curtains sweep the tragic scene
Of dusty cherished memories
Where love longed to meet.

But underneath the lonely rugs
A canvassed floor lays in wait
For a brush to mend this broken
scene by painting hearts with hope.

As warmer moments bless the space
Framing the future's looking glass
Asking pain to melt away

And leave love's charm to pass.

For the viewer has the power
To see the beauty in the room
And channel inner passion
That never really left.

Illusion caused its absence
That marked a point in time
Of desperate inner healing
Where damaged hearts were blamed.

But tender passion laid in wait
For virgin hearts to forge new ways
And mend the broken windows
For love to banish hate.

For chance reaches out
With hands of newer hope
Providing deeper meaning
Where love becomes the show.

This is what this place is for:
A home of hearts that never dies
That heals the wounds of harsher
days
To grow the love that summer
knows.

TRUTH

And 'tis my faith that every flower
Enjoys the air it breathes.

William Wordsworth

A change for life

The hands of time envelop you
Drawing lines upon your face
You read a mirrored story
Of the times you've said goodbye.

Every tear of mourning
The touch that couldn't stay
The times that shook your soul
And the hungry ache of pain.

Your face is all you know
When your past has lapsed behind
And you yearn for fuller feelings
In the empty space below.

The strength within your hands
That stems from beauty deep
Its scent is pure and special
Waiting just beneath.

But something keeps you hurting
A sound you know so well
You hear its hollow whisper
Believing all it tells.

Illusion fills your days
Destroying all your light
Until you meet your master
And make a change for life.

You owe it to your being
To wrap yourself in love
And cherish every moment
With the power that is now.

Watchful Eye

Her longing, watchful eye
Absorbs love and all the misery
In every scene she sees
In all the passers by.

Knowing what she knows
Is only present in *her* mind
Her heart still stirs beneath
For the stories she perceives.

Everyone's a mystery
Yet they are all the same
In their different daily stories
And the way they feel their pain.

Her lashes flicker droplets
As she senses all the shame
That burdens every shoulder
Of those that got away.

But her iris senses magic
From the sparkle that she sees
In the hearts of all the people
That pass her every day.

Wings of Gold

The hand that held her breath
Dulled her starlit life -
Opportune and critical
It grabbed her inner light.

Watchful was her taker
Hunting down her power
Seizing all she'd made herself
Delighting as she cowered.

Surprising was her state
When her wits fell out of bounds
She missed his cunning presence
That took her by the hand.

Her breath was lost in his
Her chest began to crack
For all the while her little heart
Was bursting to be heard.

Calling her to see what was
And take back all her worth
It cloaked her in protection
'til strength returned to her.

Freedom was her weapon
Her chosen tool of choice
But every now and then
She let it slip again.

But knowing this has taught her
That little birds move stronger free
Whispering wise just like the owl
And soaring high with eagle power.

For when she spreads her wings of
gold
Special purpose grows
To light the lives of others
Empowering as she goes.

Unapologetically

I owe not one person an apology,
excuse or my time.
But I do owe myself compassion,
forgiveness and love.

I owe not one person a promise I
cannot keep.
But I do owe myself a promise to
share the secrets that I hold *far* too
deep.

I owe not one person a lesson, a
telling or demand.
But I do owe myself change from the
lessons I have learnt.

I owe not one person my body, my
mind or my spirit.
But I do owe myself all of these, and
in return I open my heart.

We owe not one person a thing.
But we do owe ourselves to do the
right thing.

We owe ourselves everything.
And in return our hearts and minds
will rise into our being.

Nature is my Therapy

As corny as it sounds:
Nature is my therapy.

The hills, the rivers, the trees –
They all speak to me.

Deep in the valleys
And high above rock
I return to center
When the earth beckons me.

The simple things –
They truly bring joy
But locked in the hustle
We're blocked from their call.

In spite of ourselves
We run from whom we are
Before we love our nature
And listen to our souls.

The contours of our being
Match the scenic lands
But running from our essence
Keeps us distant from source.

It only takes a moment
To delve into our core

And discover who we are: to love
and adore.

Holding in our hands
A moment's drop of life
A spark from way up high
And the twinkle in her eye.

We are all and simply nothing
In the space of no time
But when we pause to listen
Our beauty shines bright.

The Moon Delights

The full moon delights
Shining bright
Upon a star blessed sky.

Filled with truth
She knows you –
She'll open up your heart.

She'll cast a spell of pure intent
With her brilliant beam of light.

Feminine and full of power
You'll feel yourself unite.

To manifest your deepest self
Despite the dark of night.

TRAVEL

I am the infinite sea, and all worlds
are but grains of sand upon my
shore.

Kahil Gibran.

Vancouver Snow

Snow amongst the palms
Beached from the north.

Sprinkles gentle offerings
Upon the city shores.

Ghosts of trees know snow well
Though not along these sands.

And though it seems absurd
It is as true as it stands.

For a blizzard filled the eye
Of a storm passing by.

And as it brushed the beach
It left snowflakes in its reach.

A Night in Manila

The clock that ticks
The cats at war
Front stoop natter
I'm awake at four.

A night in Manila
Where scooters roar
On a couch too small
My thoughts start to gnaw.

Then my giggles resound
To these absurd night sounds
As they mount in volume
The later it gets.

I just want to sleep
But one night doesn't matter
As this strange new place
Makes my mind want to chatter.

So I smile inside
In this city so new
That I won't get to know
'cause I'm passing through.

Which is strange in itself
In the grand scheme of things
But it's serving a purpose
For adventure to begin.

The Charm of Havana

Bang, crash and clang
The sounds of the sleepless night
man
He hollers to his amigo
Happy on el Ron.

Samba, jazz and reggaeton
Move sensual hips and feet
As Havana's bell tolls
To a humid, collective beat.

Hot and hungry
The city wants your CUC
As the CUP is worth little
For new hip hop dreams.

Men call and leer
'Hey pretty lady', 'you are my
flower', and place notes under coffee
cups suggesting sweet sex.

It's a mixed up city
With its own special sauce
Chaotic in flavour
And spectacularly coarse.

The children set the balance
Laughing through the streets
Posing for photos

By colours that crumble.

The pinks, greens and blues
The tourists adore the hues
As they ride along the boulevard in a
sassy classic car.

Hemingway, Hugo, Fidel and
Guevara
Coconut, pineapple and tropical
guava.

Absorbing the views
With a Cohiba or two
The sun goes down
To sensual southern sounds.

New York, My Love

The city where the sounds wake me
And send me to sleep
For they serenade me
With every passing beep.

The city that fills my heart
With awe and delight
Where my eager little eyes absorb all
of the lights.

The city where I don't care to sleep
For every corner serves a surprise
On every new visit I arrive.

The city I'll see again
Hopeful with dreams
Of a new adventure
And I'll love all that it means.

A Secret Escape

Hanging out in paradise
Friends by my side
A laugh a giggly minute
Gave me joy deep inside.

On an unexpected journey
To islands on the hide
We enjoyed simple pleasures
Strolling side-by-side.

Castaways from home
With secrets to be told
Nothing fits the mold
When the map is all you know.

Adventures at our grasp
We rode the choppy seas
Dodged electric storms
And felt the scorch of the heat.

Wandering together
With our feet unbound
The sand between our toes
We felt nature all around.

We slept beneath the stars
On precious lands afar
As we leapt to our depths
With every new turn.

Eyes wide in awe
Silent in our thoughts
We navigated friendship
To learn who we are.

A Stormy Dawn

The dawn lifts for the sun to burn
through, and a new day is drawn.

As stardust formed millennia ago,
fade behind clouds that wish to rain
again.

Speckled lightning tickles distant
lands quilted in mist.

Where warm waves pool at the
shoreline, calming the sand battered
by a stormy sea.

And though the thick air weighed
down on sleepless souls last night, it
cuddled their spirits, keeping worries
at bay that have no place in paradise.

The Power of the Rudder

Silent is the rudder
That steers a gentle path
Of floating inhibition
Over calming island seas.

But when the weather turns
The rudder takes command
To steer a line of action
Up against the storm.

Its subtle call to prayer
Is often overlooked
But when the seas are rolling fierce
The rudder meets the roar.

Fighting with the current
The route remains on track
For the rudder knows the truth
When balance is restored.

By listening to its voice
A solid line is kept
Flowing through the water
Against the trying depths.

Coursing through the tides
Courage held inside
Steering home to harbor
With a modest sense of pride.

Dolarog Skies

The moonlit sky
Releases our masks
Freeing our heavy hearts.

As the sun stands by
With a watchful eye
Melting our minds away.

Stars shoot down
Before they die
Shimmering all the way.

Then daylight dances
Upon the shores
Creating brand new chances.

As the trees call
With a gentle voice
Calming all that's harmed.

For nature states
That the past is the past
Soothing every second.

As the leaves turn
With a better vision
Providing a new beginning.

The Gift of the Beach

Soft is the sand
Cushioning my feet
I sink so deep
That my heart slows its beat.

Heaven beneath
Within my reach
My mind goes to sleep
As I merge with the beach.

Afterword

Desire is an inspired feeling that has the power to transform. Without it we remain stagnant and detached from our wants and needs.

How we transform desire into something that serves you and others, is where the magic of choice reigns in.

We can choose to do things that benefit, support and lift others and ourselves up or we can opt to do the opposite.

From my earlier book titled *Desire*, I share again my favourite poem: Grace Knows. I believe it captures the choice of pushing through rather than giving up, and supporting others to succeed when they're struggling. The poem was inspired by a night on a mountain when a group of people came together to raise funds for others.

We all need support, whether it looks like it on the outside or not.

Every single day offers an opportunity to choose kindness in our dealings with others, to choose love over hate, and to choose to do the caring and compassionate thing.

It takes only a second to interrupt yourself if you're about to lash out, turn away or judge harshly.

The simple way to do this is to take a breath.

Although breathing is one of the most natural things we do, it is often the thing we forget to do when it matters most.

And yet choosing to take a breath that cuts through a hurtful reaction is essential to a more positive impact on others.

What we need more than anything in this world is for people to know they matter. Nobody needs to be told they don't, as this simply is not true.

I hope you know how much you matter in this world, and how much meaning you bestow. You matter no less than your neighbor or the person you perceive to be better than you.

Always know how important you are.

Grace Knows.

Grace Knows

A touch of grace kept the rain away,
as I walked to the call of the summit:
stepping through the dark of the
night lit by a haloed moon.

A cooling breeze on a balmy night
fluttered gentle relief, but only a
mantra could ease the chatter of my
wandering monkey mind.

As my heart took charge of this
difficult path, the skies rejoiced with
a shooting star: when the mind is free
it truly believes, in all that it sets out
to be.

Breathing life into my legs, their
strength rose to the challenge,
finding success at the imposing crest
in the midst of a raging storm.

My mind prepared for the long
descent still darkened by the night, as
a seemingly endless journey can take
its mental toll.

And just when I thought I had
nothing left, I was asked to give
some more, as a stranger's hand

reached out to mine in desperation's
want.

Step-by-step we shared my light to
safely wander home, 'til the sun
came up and we smiled to ourselves,
as we knew we were free there on.

By sharing light we saw our way far
from a darkened heart, and met our
challenge until the end to dance with
the breaking day.

Final Thoughts & Thanks

I want to acknowledge the great work that people do in this world to assist the wellbeing of others. Whether a person is a paid professional or volunteers to help another doesn't matter. What's important is that someone benefits from their input.

Supporting mental health is dear to my heart, and one of the reasons I studied psychology at university. As my Mum is a therapist, I am also inspired by the way she helps people to transform their lives for the better.

The work of the Samaritans and the various charities that have been set up to support the mental and physical wellbeing of people, make such a difference to those in need.

I have a particular fondness for the support provided by Mind charity. Its impact is vast, some of which I have witnessed in people close to my heart. I have therefore decided to donate all profits from this book in its first year of publication to this worthy cause.

The mental wellbeing of young people is also dear to my heart. It is for this reason that I have opted to reduce the price of my two Benjamin Frank books, so that I no longer earn profit from them.

Not only does this support literacy levels in children from lower household incomes, but the messages in the books will land in the hands of more children also. Benjamin Frank doesn't find life easy, and throughout the books I have subtly interwoven techniques to help him. It has always been my hope that children, who struggle like him, can use the books to help them cope with similar difficulties. The more children I can help, the more my mission is accomplished.

And to the people in my life:

Thank you, as always to my parents and my brother. They continually have my back, and the older I get the more I appreciate how lucky I am.

To my amazing friends, from the cats with a K, to the ducks and flamingos, you are all truly awesome. You have all helped me verbalise the words that have sometimes been difficult for me to say. You make me giggle until my belly hurts, and have joined me on my various adventures close to home and far away.

Of course, when adventure fills your world, it's important that someone always knows where you are. Technology allows my family to track me when I'm travelling to remote islands during times of earthquakes and typhoons. But I've also had to enlist a next of kin on home soil. Rhia, you are my rock. Thank you for monitoring the 'Bat line' for the many activities I sign up for. I can't promise I'll slow down, but maybe I'll let you know after the event from now on.

And to those of you that have indulged me with my list of forty things I wanted to do before I turned forty. Whether we've flown somewhere together, tried a new activity together or eaten somewhere delicious, thank you for being there with me.

To Ben, your art is awesome, and I love that your work inspired *Watchful Eye*. Thank you also for giving me a roof when I needed it.

And extended thanks go to everyone who offered me a place to stay when my living arrangements fell apart.

I am also eternally grateful for all the opportunities that have graced my life. The new experiences I have been afforded and the people I have met have been astounding.

Which brings me onto the things... the happenings... that I cannot explain. Whether a barrier was removed at just the right time or a gift of sorts appeared when I needed it, thank you.

I've learnt that these things appear when I let life happen rather than force it. Versus when I've tried to control things too much, and life hasn't worked out so well.

Listening to the difference between flow and control has always helped me make the right decision, even if that is to admit I feel out of control and need the help of others to get me through.

And finally, I'd like to acknowledge all of your struggles. To those of you that get up every day in spite of it all, and to all of you that can't get up today.

Although today is just a day, it sometimes seems long and painful. And when you feel that way you are probably right. You are also right when you notice it disappear in a flash. But, however long or fleeting each day seems, you and your needs always matter. Whether those needs are the basics, such as, water, sleep, food or shelter. Whether you need to motivate yourself to take on a challenge or find the support you need to realize a goal or face a difficult time in your life, every moment counts.

Each day serves us up something new. Whether you receive a good

serving or not, you have a choice.
And whatever you choose to do,
please look after yourself and others.

Much Love,
Marie

The Author

Marie Skilling has previously published two poetry books and two children's adventure stories. All of her work is inspired by her life and travels, and the heartfelt perceptions she feels as she observes life. It is important to Marie to write in a way that resonates with people to meet a need in them when facing difficulties. This book is no different. It is her hope that she touches the heart of every person that reads her words, and they feel inspired to do great things for themselves and others.

Marie was raised in South West London and has lived in Australia and Canada. She studied psychology at university, has trained as a yoga teacher and coach, and writing is her lifelong passion.